C000171790

HIPPY VALLEY
(a secret history)

Copyright © George Murphy 2018

The right of George Murphy to be identified as the author of this book has been asserted by him in accordance with the Copyright, Designs and Patents Act 1998.

All rights reserved.

All rights reserved. No part of this publication may be reproduced, stored in or introduced into a retrieval system or transmitted, in any form, or by any means (electronic, mechanical, photocopying, recording or otherwise) without the prior written permission of the publisher or unless such copying is done under a current Copyright Licensing Agency license. Any person who does any unauthorised act in relation to this publication may be liable to criminal prosecution and civil claims for damages.

HIPPY VALLEY
(a secret history)

Monologues and songs

written and performed by

GEORGE MURPHY

First Published in 2018 by Fantastic Books Publishing
Cover design by Gabi

ISBN (ebook): 978-1-912-053-81-0
ISBN (paperback): 978-1-912-053-80-3

Foreword

Music Hall humour was often bawdy, but rarely explicit. As Dr Jonathan Miller once said, when he dropped by for a brew, having boundaries can make humour funnier. The most common question I'm asked after a gig is 'How d'you remember all that?' Sometimes followed by, 'When's your book coming out then?' So here it is.

The setting is the Upper Calder Valley around Hebden Bridge, an old mill town that has transformed itself into 'one of the hippest places on the planet'. The area overlaps what Sally Wainwright, in her TV Cop Series, has called Happy Valley. For me it started with the notion that Albert Einstein, being a clever sort of a feller, might once have stayed in Hebden, taking advantage of a cheap B&B offer, whilst most folks were away to Blackpool on their annual Wakes' Week holiday. Now during his stay, happen young Albert tipped off a local joiner, drinking partner and amateur Music Hall performer about how to make a Time Travel Machine. This chap, Mr Herbert Bradley Makepiece, has since become my muse, tipping me off about changes for good and bad across the decades. So really, it's Herbert you need to congratulate or complain to after reading this here Secret History.

I've often performed alongside Rod Dimbleby, a proper Yorkshireman and a teller of dialect tales, especially from our recent past. He tells me that in traditional Yorkshire dialect writing aitches are dropped in t' telling, not in t' spelling. So think on!

George Murphy,
Hebden Bridge, 2018

Acknowledgements

Some of these stories and songs appeared in an ebook, compiled with Chris Ratcliffe, Editor of HebWeb, the first news and features webpage in the country. Pam Dimbleby has added musical notation to some of my tunes and these can be found on my *Murphy's Monologues* website. Many thanks to event organisers who have kindly invited me to perform these tales in venues large and small and to the audiences who have paid to laugh at me! Finally, to Kath (aka My Present Wife) for her help in so many ways, especially for providing the first audience for most of these stories.

Contents

Secret History

Now a friend of a friend,
Of this friend that I know,
Has a nephew in t' C.I.D.
And he told his uncle
Who then told his friend
Who told my friend,
And he told me:
It's all a conspiracy!

He said his cop shop's got miles
Of these underground aisles …
And one's stacked full of piles
Of these top secret files.
Well, his job is compiling
A list of this filing,
Entitled, 'A Secret History'.

Well, this fuzz is no fool,
He stayed on at school,
He's got two GCSEs!
But he trusted his uncle,
Who trusted his friend,
Who trusted my friend,
Who trusts me,

'Bout these files that he happened to see.
So, now I'm going to trust thee …

Part One: Trouble on t' Tops

The Todmorden Triangle

(Reports suggest that slight rises in the local birth rate occur
following sightings of UFOS in the Todmorden area)

Gordon had a calm demeanour,
Rarely had he been serener,
Night time driving over t' Valley,
One hand steering – casually –
Unaware, so he worn't bothered,
Overhead a Space Ship hovered.
But Gordon didn't want for nowt,
Until his engine just cut out …

This circumstance made Gordon groan.
But when he tried his mobile phone
And found that that had also quit,
He gave three buggers, one Brad Pitt!
When sudden luminosity
Aroused his curiosity …
A dazzling light inspired his awe
And Gordon opened t' driver's door.

If we'd been there, we all would shout,
'For god's sake, Gordon … don't get out!'
For we all know, though he forgot,
Round here's a UFO hotspot.
And joggers, doggers, cows and cops,
Have all been rounded up on t' tops.
But in a trance, as if instructed,
Ginger Gordon wor abducted!

Now, every sci-fi student knows,
Space aliens watch our TV shows.
And Gordon's lot had special powers
To make their features look like ours.
And one, that knew soap operas well,
Transformed into a Femme Fatale,
Stood first in line, Gordon to greet,
As Gail from Coronation Street!

What happened next his mind repressed …
Though tabloid journalists have guessed
That, driven by some desperate need,
Gail and Gordon did the deed!
Despite this speculation tawdry,
No one spoke to his wife, Audrey.
Until, at her car maintenance class
She told her secrets to Our Lass.

When Gordon One went off on t' drive,
Another Gordon had arrived!
Identical in every way …
Except, he asked about her day!
And after bleeding t' radiators,
Made coq au vin wi' mashed potatoes,
But only winked when she demanded,
'Gordon, how come tha'rt left handed?'

That Gordon had his wicked way,
By use of summat called 'foreplay'…
And Audrey thrilled at each sensation,
Especially t' use of levitation!

That night, when Gordon One returned
With stories of what he had learned
About celebrities from space,
Audrey tried to keep straight faced.
For inside her – all a jingling –
Wor two genomes, intermingling!

And nine months later, Gord and Aud
Announced t' birth of daughter Maude.
Now three years old wi' auburn locks,
Pink of cheeks and dress and socks.
And Gordon says, with certainty,
'My daughter's dead spit of me!'
And asks said toddler what she thinks,
And Maude looks at her mum … and winks!

So, those as wor born near Stoodley Pike,
Should pay full heed to this story:
Tha might be one part Lancastrian,
One part Tyke …
And one part Alpha Centauri!
And on some world in Outer Space,
A child – with Gail from Corrie's face –
Has started off a Ginger Race.

Author's note: For further revelations, type 'Todmorden and UFOs'
into your search engine. Tod straddles the Yorkshire/Lancashire
border and Stoodley Pike is a monument, high above the town.

Frank's Ramble

When Frank went rambling up on t' moors,
His venture seemed romantic,
But then a heavy mist came down …
Now Frank wor feeling frantic.

He'd got no signal on his phone,
And day had turned to night
And mist had blanked out moon and stars,
But then Frank saw a light.

A coach lamp hung beside a door,
But t' house wor dark and shuttered.
'IS ANYBODY HOME?' he shouts,
'To ring for t' taxi?' mutters.

Three times he raps upon that door …
Faint echoes each recall.
But as he turns to walk away,
Sharp footsteps resound in t' hall.

And t' door opens to dazzling light,
Frank thinks himself inspected.
'Who is it my dear?' a voice enquires,
'It's he whom we expected!'

Frank follows her, as if in thrall,
Mumbling apologies.
But as he turns into t' front room,
He's shocked at what he sees.

He looks at one face, then at t' other.
Then 'Lord have mercy!' he begs.
No eyes, no nose, no mouths at all.
Their faces are smooth … as eggs!

He stands transfixed before them both.
Then he hears an inner yell.
He concentrates, then hears more clear …
And t' words are, 'Run like hell!'

He staggers off down t' dazzling hall,
And sprints down t' gravel track.
And plunges into mist and moor,
And never once looks back!

But on some lonely moorland path,
Dipped headlights, at last, he spots.
And Frank strides out on t' tarmac road,
And t' car slows down … and stops.

T' car's engine purrs as they set off,
Frank states his destination,
In time, his hooded driver asks,
'What caused your perturbation?'

Relaxing then, Frank tells his tale.
And t' driver listens, intently.
Then, smoothly slowing t' car to stop,
'No features at all?' asks gently.

When Frank turns to his rescuer,
His courage leaks its last dreg.
No eyes, no nose, no mouth at all:
His face as smooth … as an egg!

Author's Note: this plot comes from an untraced 'pulp fiction' novel that reportedly diverted the Bloomsbury group one sunny afternoon in the 1920s.

A Monologue About a Bog

(Early in our history,
When everyone spoke Welsh,
It should be no mystery,
They'd twenty words for 'squelch!'
For when thick mist descended,
Folks sometimes went off course,
And they'd be found upended,
In t' blanket bog on t' moors.

But t' Romans hated roamin',
They just walked in straight lines.
Happen they worn't at home in
Our 'Northern Apennines',
For, marching through our region,
They wouldn't take detours,
That's how they lost t' 9th Legion,
In t' blanket bog on t' moors …)

Back when times wor chivalrous,
T' authorities didn't quibble,
If boggarts, most carnivorous,
Sometimes had a nibble.
A traveller strayed from t' springy heath,
Then heard demonic roars …
Soon his bones lay underneath,
In t' blanket bog on t' moors.

But when a lord wor exercising,
His favourite hunting horse,
And t' Boggart, materialising,
Ate a double course,
Nobles said in consternation,
'We'll have to write new laws,
T' Boggart's bit above his station,
In t' blanket bog on t' moors!'

When an Alternative Witch,
By name, Morgan La Fay,
With spells for bog and ditch,
(She lived down Hebden way),
Said, 'Probiotic yoghurt
And other natural cures,
Will pacify that boggart
In t' blanket bog on t' moors!'

T' Boggart, all crepuscular,
At twilight left his lair,
Returning, big and muscular,
Found Morgan, sat in t' chair.
'Ah know tha needs, old Butch,' quoth she.
'My supper!' he guffaws.
'No! What tha need's a woman's touch,
In t' blanket bog on t' moors!'

And then that witch contrarian,
Through spells and incantations,
Turned him vegetarian,
But don't tell his relations!

T' next spell she cast for heavy sleep,
(Some say they've heard his snores),
Used clever trick of counting sheep,
In t' blanket bog on t' moors.

And right through t' next millennium,
A thousand shears of fleece,
With pleasant dreams about his mum,
He slept through war and peace.
Till underground he heard a sound
Of revving 4 by 4s,
And his disturbance wor profound,
In t' blanket bog on t' moors.

For bulldozers wor digging gunge,
On t' orders o't new boss.
'This bog is like a massive sponge,
Let's burn off sphagnum moss.'
But after burning, loss of heat,
And t' Boggart knew what caused
Him having frozen hands and feet,
In t' blanket bog on t' moors.

And to t' new owners of our moors
T' Government gave great wealth,
'For improving The Great Outdoors,
In time for The Glorious Twelfth.'
And some o't bog wor burned and drained,
But fear made t' workers pause.
And t' Boggart's warren still remained,
In t' blanket bog on t' moors!

Now what goes up, must come down,
So with evaporation,
And folks down in all t' valley towns
Received an inundation!
First one flood, then another
Broke through each water course,
But t' Boggart stayed down under cover,
In t' blanket bog on t' moors.

For generations, as tha knows,
In mills and houses and shops,
Folks had dealt with overflows
Wi' extra supply of mops.
But wi' this global warming
Floods filled up all t' ground floors
And minds turned non conforming,
To t' blanket bog on t' moors …

But just as t' sense o' grievance nagged,
Came t' news o t' record kill:
A shooting party: Boggart bagged!
High up on Boggart Hill!
Most said, it's what t' hunters deserved
And t' Boggart felt no remorse,
For each hunter wor well preserved …
In t' blanket bog on t' moors!

As t' Inspector said, at local station -
T' hunters' families to sweeten –
'Except in terms of Education,
None of them wor EATEN!'*

And then laughter he stifled,
A credit to t' local force,
When asked where t' Boggart shoved all t' rifles –
And did he shout, 'Up yours!?'

And don't dismiss this fantasy,
Because folklore and mystery
Connect us to our history.
And back down t' hill
Each Jack and Jill –
Shopkeepers with empty tills,
Homeowners with insurance bills
And waiters who'd stopped earning –
Said, "That's our bog they're burning!
And scientists with detailed log,
And you and I are going to dog
All those who desecrate our bog!

*The Inspector subsequently took early retirement.

Author's Note: the boggart in this tale shares the monstrous proportions and predatory characteristics of the Scandinavian troll. Boggarts who lose their traditional habitat appear in folk lore as shrunken, mischievous and shape shifting tricksters. It is considered bad luck to say the given name of a boggart.

Part Two: T' Bad Old Days

A Man of Few Words

Prince Vince wor handsome, quite a catch,
And yet he'd never made his match.
For lasses spurned him as their choice,
'Cos he loved t' sound of his own voice.

A passing Witch, who thought him cute,
Decided she'd prefer him mute.
And cast a spell that cost him dear,
To only say one word per year!

Next Feast Day, this dumbstruck feller,
Took a shine to t' storyteller,
Who told a bold and saucy tale,
And said her name wor Emma Dale.
And he thought on, at next year's do,
He'd happen say a word … or two.

But next year he wor proper smitten,
She had him purring like a kitten.
But because o' t Witch's spell,
He'd need three years his love to tell.
Oh, Peripatetic Performer …
He loved her, but couldn't inform her!

But after those three years had passed,
Our Prince's lips remained shut fast.
His mind had turned to t' marriage state,
Now four more years he'd have to wait.

Four words he'd need at his disposal,
For proposing his proposal.

Till nine years after t' Witch's spell,
T' day came at last his love to tell.
After t' Feast Day cakes and ale,
A shout went up for 'Emma Dale!'
Once more her audience wor wowed,
She blew them kisses, scraped and bowed.

Then t' Prince came forrard, full of charm,
And gently took her slender arm.
And led her out to t' balcony,
Where t' Royal Gardens she could see.
Accompanied by t' songs o t' birds,
He uttered his nine precious words.

'My darling, I love you. Will you marry me?'
And, slowly turning back from t' garden,
Smiling sweetly, she said …
'Pardon?'

Author's note: this was inspired by a joke in *Plato and a platypus walk into a bar; understanding philosophy through jokes* (2016), by Klein and Cathcart.

Uncle Herbert's Machine

'This pub,' said our local Landlady,
Once accommodated Franz Josef Lizst!'
I said, 'What about Brahms?
Did he succumb to its charms?'
When an old chap behind me said, 'Pssst …

Never mind talk of fancy Composers,
Or offcumdens of mighty renown,
Whilst tha drinks that sherbet,
I'll tell of a Herbert
As wor born and brought up in this town.

There have been some amazing inventions,
But t' greatest invention I've seen,
Wor in 1905,
I wor first one to drive,
Uncle Herbert's Time Travel Machine!

T' contraption wor not much to look at,
Two seats, and some levers and gears,
And a set of dials,
Not for counting miles,
But to show distance travelled in years.

Uncle said, 'Will tha be my co-pilot?'
And he helped me to set Target Date.
So I gave dials a tweak,
Month, year and week,
And it stopped at 1968.

Now Mother wor quite disconcerted.
She said, 'Don't fetch him back late for his tea.'
But Uncle just laughed,
He said, 'Don't talk so daft!
Think on Einstein's Relativity.'

So we waved goodbye to all t' family,
And smoothly moved up to top gear.
And to my surprise,
When I opened my eyes,
We'd leapt forrard, 63 year!

When all dust and smoke had quite settled,
I couldn't believe what I saw.
It worn't room I know,
No carpets or lino,
Just cavemen, sat round on our floor.

All t' men had hair down to t' shoulders,
And passed round an old cigarette,
And lasses' short skirts,
Fair upset Uncle Bert,
It's a scene I shall never forget.

Then t' leader o t' cavemen came forrard,
Wearing bear skins, a right proper mess.
'Good trip man,' he said,
Then, shaking his head,
'What's tha doing in that Fancy Dress?'

Happen Uncle wor proper offended,
For pushing on t' levers right hard,
We leapt forrard 50 year,
All t' way in top gear,
And landed outside in t' back yard.

Then Uncle stared up at t' mill chimneys,
Saying, 'Look lad, no smoke's coming out!'
And all down our street,
Folks worn't using their feet,
Horseless carriages took them about!

An' some dined at pavement cafes,
Or cruised on t' canal in a barge.
And t' best thing of all,
Wor this hole in t' bank wall,
That wor givin' out cash, free o' charge!

'By … this is alright,' said my uncle,
But we promised we'd get back for tea.
And when we reappeared,
All t' family cheered,
For my Uncle Herbert and me.

But nobbut three days later –
I'll tell thee summat that's weird –
Uncle Bert had a date
Wi' t' barmaid's best mate
An' both of them an' t' machine disappeared.

Still, there's been some amazing inventions,
But t' greatest invention I've seen,
Wor in 1905,
I wor first one to drive,
Uncle Herbert's Time Travel Machine.'

Author's note: Liszt stayed for one night at The White Lion pub in
Hebden Bridge during a successful tour of the British Isles.

The Yorkshire Don Juan

(Here's a tale regarding fashion a la mode,
'Bout a salesman who broke The Salesman's Code.
Though some customers are kissable,
Kissing em's dismissible:
When work an' pleasure meet …
Allus be discreet!)

I left my Yorkshire home one fateful day,
For a salesman's job on t' streets of Liverpool.
But not long out of school,
T' sales team tret me like a fool,
And had me sellin', every day, ladies' slippers and lingerie!

I met two merchant seamen set to sale,
And asked what they missed most when out at sea.
T' Small Un said, 'Dis ale!
But, sometimes – in a gale –
I miss me Mrs and me Mrs misses me.'

So we had a toast to their fidelity.
And Tall Un says, 'Dat's true that, I agree.
We've got girls in every port,
And although we don't go short,
I miss da kisses dat me Mrs gives to me!'

So I told them that I sold from door to door
Such items as a Mrs might be missin',
Special stuff for t' bottom drawer …
But sometimes they wanted more.

And I really made them listen, when I started reminiscing
'Bout this Mrs I'd been kissin'.

'She's a reet big lass that lives on Daisy Street.
She wears size 10 slippers –
An' those slippers are reet full of feet.
In a flannelette nightie, she looks like Aphrodite.
An' when that big Mrs kisses, I really knows what bliss is!'

But t' Small Seaman started to repeat:
'She wears size 10 slippers and she lives on Daisy Street?
She gets flighty in a well upholstered nighty …?
Dat's my Mrs giving kisses in dem slippers
And dat nighty was a treat!'

T' atmosphere in t' Mermaid Inn grew tense …
I said, 'Ooh … *that's* a coincidence!'
But t' Tall Un said, 'Before you do him in,
Your Mrs is a twin … It's complicated dis is –
Dat twin lives near your Mrs …
Perhaps he never kissed her – perhaps he kissed her sister!'

A fog horn sounded mournful out on t' Mersey,
As t' Small Un came up close – nose to nose.
My heart wor poundin' in my jersey –
I knew I'd get no mercy.
He said, 'The question is:
Was that flanellated Mrs,
Giving kisses in dem slippers, Rose or Liz?'

Now, questioned under oath,
I would have answered, 'Both.'
Instead, I pondered, where did t' Small Un plight his troth?
Then I took a gambler's chance …
And I chose, 'Rose!'

T' Small Un said, 'That's grim …
I'm married to Liz … but Rose is married to him!'
An t' Tall Un shook his fist, saying,
'Do you want some of dis?
My biggest wish is to feed you to da fishes!'

But t' Small Un says, 'It's alright son, we're joking!
There's something about a salesman that's provoking.
Our wives are quite petite,
They've not got size 10 feet!
But dose twin sisters, giving kisses in dem slippers,
Were once … Misters!'

I said to t' Small Un, 'Run that past me again!'
He said, 'Rose and Liz of Daisy Street,
Were once called Reg and Len.
You think you're a Yorkshire Don Ju-in,
But you don't know what you're doing!'
And after many more jibes at me,
Those Seamen went back to t' sea.

So, enjoy your kisses while they last.
Here's a toast both strong and tender:
To every lad and every lass –
And those who swap their gender!

Author's note: an earlier version of this tale appears in *Make 'em laugh!* a website that also contains many famous examples of Music Hall monologues and songs.

Fiery Jack

(After t' war, some posh folks in our nation,
Decided to install refrigeration.
Freezers came into fashion,
Whilst most folks had to ration,
Thus preserving upper classes from starvation.

Here's a bawdy tale entitled Fiery Jack,
'A deep heat treatment for pains in joints and back'.
But, as every careful customer understands,
After each application, be sure to wash your hands!)

A Kitchen Maid with an infatuation,
Decided to take charge o' t situation.
That kitchen had some gin in,
To fortify her sinning,
A set of keys and jars of embrocation.

At dead of night she stole into a room,
Hoping to seduce a handsome Groom.
But drinkers now will pardon her,
That room belonged to t' Gardener,
An ancient Flower of England past full bloom.

His big white eyes stared out at her from t' black.
She said, 'I've done a damage to me back.'
An' he wor right impressed
When she lifted up her vest
An' said, 'It needs a rub wi Fiery Jack!'

From t' window's pale moon light, with spinnin' head,
She stumbled cross his floor to his dark bed.
T' old gardener took her tub
And he give her back a rub,
But then she whispered, 'Now do t' front instead!'

Then Walter up and bolted out o' t door …
Though not much later he came back for more.
But consequence wor boring,
T' Kitchen Maid wor snoring
And Walter despised himself and swore.

Whilst she slept, old Walter held her tight,
Waiting for next morning's breaking light.
When round her front her reached …
But she leapt up and SCREECHED!
An' poor old Walter cowered back wi' fright.

He said, 'Hush thissen, or else we'll both get t' sack!'
She said, 'Tha hands are flaming covered with FIERY JACK!'
When she saw she'd slept wi' Walter,
Her fury didn't falter,
She pummelled him about both head and back.

Now this commotion had woken t' handsome Groom,
Who padded cross to t' door of his own room.
Where he saw a sight bewitching
As Mabel ran to t' kitchen,
Wailing like a banshee facing doom!

So he follows her to t' kitchen, then he sees her:
Standing almost naked next to t' freezer,
Showing sheer delight she'd got 'em,
Frozen peas clutched to front bottom,
He felt a surge of passion then to seize her.

First, he'd heard her shout his name. Then here in t' larder,
She wor usin' frozen peas to cool her ardour!
Oh, how blind he'd been,
Such love he'd never seen!
How much his cold indifference must have scarred her!

Frank moved towards her, but Mabel frozed,
She said, 'Jack, I'm temporarily indisposed.'
Jack didn't mean to be alarming,
And like a right Prince Charming,
He fell down on one knee and he proposed!

Author's note: this story is built up from an anecdote told more than 30 years ago to my wife and I by Jack Noble of Cottonstones.

That's Bob All Over

(*A Taste of Honey, A Kind of Loving, This Sporting Life and so forth, said, 'Eee but it's Grim up North!'*)

Pregnant, wi nowt in her purse –
Some things are worse than The Curse …
'Head, shoulders, knees and toes …'
From a school she can hear an old song,
And quietly she sings along …
'And eyes and …'

Picture Bob's eyes …
He couldn't disguise his surprise
When he happened to greet her –
And she asked for a bob for her meter.

And then there's his ears –
Though he'd had them for years –
Heard her sobs in his bedsit above her …
And he wondered if nobody loved her.

And think of Bob's nose,
That awoke from repose
When t' fragrances rose of bread making …
Although midnight's a strange time for baking.

And mustachioed lips,
That drank tiny sips,
Although t' nips that she quaffed wor much neater –
When he called round to fix her old heater.

And consider Bob's chest,
Against which she pressed
And confessed that her husband had beat her.
And Bob wondered if life would defeat her.

Also his belly,
Full of custard and jelly,
Celebrating our Queen's Coronation,
When they called for 'Three cheers for our nation!'

Below that's his groin,
That did briefly conjoin with her loins.
But she made him feel bad –
When she said he looked just like her dad!

So he settled for teas –
With a tray on his knees –
And a big slice of cheese an' some ham …
Till t' day that she mentioned a pram.

And picture Bob's feet,
As he ran down t' back street.
Not as fleet as her husband who caught her –
And pinned her down in t' coat Bob bought her.

Then imagine Bob's hand,
Round a large rock spanned …
But she stabbed the man that she married,
With a knife that she always carried.

So what of their necks
And where did t' rope flex?
Well, Bob smashed in t' skull as she plunged in t' knife.
But her womb wor full – so t' Judge spared her life.

'Head, shoulders, knees and …'
That song had gone round and round in her head,
Like a needle stuck in its groove …
But then she felt Bob's baby move.

Author's note: inspired by the gritty 'Northern Novels' and black and white films of the late 50s and early 60s and my memory of walking to primary school on the morning they hanged James Hanratty.

Part Three: Hippy Valley

Teepee City

There once was a chap called Pete Farquhar,
Who wrote off his Pa's Jaguar car.
His old man threw out
That long haired roustabout,
But his Ma said, 'That's going too far, Pa!'

So Pete said, 'I've made a faux pas, Pa.
But it's alright, I'm leaving – ta ta, Ma –
For Teepee City,
With a girl most pretty,
Who's got her own mini … ha ha.'

So Pete drove north with Ophelia,
In a car painted with psychedelia,
To a tent like a fridge,
Just outside Hebden Bridge
With a suit case of rock memorabilia.

Teepee City – next morning revealed –
Was some tents and a tap in a field.
After washing alfresco,
They drove ten miles to Tesco.
'This isn't the good life!' she squealed.

Ophelia left early one day.
But Pete had decided he'd stay.
In late night carouses
He'd asked about houses –
And round here they gave them away.

For the hippy life gave Pete cold feet,
But he'd got a Great Aunt he'd kept sweet.
And you never say 'can't'
If you've got a rich aunt,
And soon Pete had bought half a street!

But though he owned houses and cars,
Pete's heart was still covered in scars.
He asked his guru
what to do,
to undo
his hoodoo,
And he said, 'Watch where you put your Rs!'

Northern Elocution Song
(Sings)
For there might be a Simple Solution,
With this lesson on Our Elocution:
For here's how to be a Wise Owl,
To whit: to woo with Flat Vowels …

(Chorus)
So …
Don't put your Rs in parth
They'll just think you're having a larf,
It's time to renounce the way you pronounce,
If you put your Rs in t' barth,
But, if you're on the path to romance,
And you think that you might have a chance …
If you're having a glass with a northern lass,
Don't put your Rs in t' glarss!

Now, they might want a slice of your bread,
Some lasses like dough, it's been said.
But, for your staff of life's sake,
You should know this …
Try to sound like an advert for Hovis.

(Chorus)
So …
Don't put your Rs in parth
They'll just think you're having a larf,
It's time to renounce the way you pronounce,
If you put your Rs in t' barth,
But, if you're on the path to romance,
And you think that you might have a chance,
If you're having a glass with a northern lass,
Don't put your Rs in t' glarss!

Now they might love your every particle,
If you drop t' definite article.
But if your loving action's still sparse,
Be careful where you put your Rs!

(Chorus)
So … (etc.)

Author's note: only some of the hippies were posh and wealthy,
but housing was cheap after the collapse of the textile industry.

Nymphs! (and Buskers Come Away!)

(In this small Pennine town where we live,
Our religion's gone alternative.
We say rivers and trees
Have their own deities
And we worship all t' beauty they give …)

Now, there's not many people's seen nymphs,
Except in museums – on plinths.
But if they want to see 'um,
Outside a museum,
They should drive around here for a glimpse.

Now, they know about nymphs – and their mania –
From Greece to Mesopotamia,
But Nymphs Anglo Saxon
Got just as much action …
That's why our nymphs chose to remain here.

Now I wouldn't tell this to Reporters,
But nymphs still inhabit our waters.
I know for a fact –
On a rolling contract –
Are Nixie* the Nymph and her daughters.

It's buskers they like to attract.
But each cull is done with great tact.
Our nymphs say, 'You're so cool!'
To each amplified fool,
Then wrap amp lead around t' vocal tract …

But you don't need to witness this "crime".
Nymphs sneak through a snicket in time.
As you sip your latte –
At some riverside cafe –
They take out young men in their prime.

Some say it's a monstrosity that young men's curiosity at nymphs' voluptuosity should lead to such atrocity. But I just shake my head an' shrug, say, 'If they cared about our lugs, and amplifiers they'd unplug, then would-be Dylans and Jake Buggs might get more generosity!'

*Nixie was the Anglo Saxon term for nymphs.

Why the Sirens Stopped Singing
(or, Fishing for Nymphs)

A Mini Opera

[SETTING: Lumb Falls, Hardcastle Crags]

NARRATOR
(*This story recalls when nymphs at Lumb Falls*
With their siren song could ignite passions strong …
Nymphs loved young men, if they could catch 'um.
Then they loved them again, then despatched 'um!
These rum goings on seem properer set to classical music and
opera …)

[Orchestra strikes up The Sirens Song – to the tune of *The Blue Danube*.

Enter: Soprano nymphs, partly submerged, essaying graceful breaststrokes]

NYMPHS* (singing)
Our beauty is rare – Come in! Come in!
And we're very bare – Come in! Come in!
Oh, don't be afraid – Come in! Come in!
No, we're not mermaids – Come in! Come in!
Your passion won't fail – Come in! Come in!
We've not got fishtails – Come in! Come in!
And then we will go with the flow …
And we'll show you all we know!

[Enter: Woodsman, agog]

NARRATOR
They got a young Woodsman besotted.
An' then they went for his carotid.
In a watery embrace,
Passion spread 'cross his face.
He wor lured, then loved, then garrotted!

[Exit: Nymphs, carrying Woodsman. Enter: Poachers' widows, unscrolling petition]

Poachers' wives lost men in addition,
And they got up a humble petition:

POACHERS' WIVES
With their senses confounded,
Our men were all drownded –
In most compromising positions!

[Exit: Widows, distraught. Enter: three bachelors, meanly apparelled]

NARRATOR
Then three bachelors: Tom, Dick and Harry –
Past their best, with no time to tarry –
Said they'd risk debauchery,
An' t' fast track to t' mortuary,
For a chance of a catch they could marry!

Next morning – across t' water skimming –
Those stout hearted lads swam wit' women.
They'd stuffed their ears full
Wi' tar and rams' wool,
Thus preventing their senses from dimming.

[Orchestra plays an extract from *The Overture to The Barber of Seville*. Brothers disrobe and dive into pool, essaying doggy paddles]

TOM
(Splashing! ... Sings)
I think I've got one!
She's got a strop on!
A captivating Naiad with no top on!
She won't give in to me,
But I'll show sympathy.
Come on then lass –
For thee an' me wor meant to be!

(Splashing!)

NARRATOR (Sings)
Soon Dick, his brother,
Had grabbed another!
Her beauty wor quite t' equal to that other!
With an almighty mighty yank,
He hauled her on to t' bank,
And said ...

DICK
I'll be your your soul mate
And your lover!
(Splashing!)

NARRATOR (Sings)
Then t' youngest brother –
Grabbed hold o't mother!
But she wor different challenge he'd discover.
For she wor much too strong …
And she kneed him in t' thong …!
And swam away before he could recover!

And so, thanks to t' plan they had hatched,
Two o t' brothers wor matched.
Though young Harry would say,
T' biggest catch got away!
Crying …

HARRY
Infamy! Infamy …!

[Moves Centre Stage]

I've not got a nymph for me!

NARRATOR
But one mornin' when out on a ride
Dick's nymph jumped in a cesspit an' died

[Exit to large splash…in lower register]

And Dick – in his hurry –
Fell into t' same slurry.

[Ditto]

An' they were interred … side by side.

From water Tom kept his nymph away –
For t' requisite year and one day –
An' their offspring, day tripping,
All loved skinny dipping –
A tradition that lasts till this day!

[Exit Narrator, disrobing]

*The Siren Song should be performed by either:
1. Burlesque artistes, accompanied by a small orchestra, with members of the council Watch Committee in attendance,
Or
2. A monologue performer in a wig.

Author's note: Lumb Falls is a famous beauty spot in Crimsworth Valley, and for many years it has been a popular venue for skinny dipping.

Coming Out Day

A fairytale

(Sings)
It wor t' best type o' weather,
An t' best time o' year,
An t' best time o' day without doubt.
All t' flowers wor bloomin'
In t' bluebell woods,
On t' day our Jane came out.

At a pantomime, she felt rapture and joy,
But this memory, our Jane had suppressed:
When she'd fallen for t' Principal Boy,
Although she wor sure he had breasts.

Later on we had other thrills,
We used to rush out to watch t' flames,
When mill owners burnt down their mills,
To fiddle insurance claims.

But then a woman had opened a shop,
With books of a Sapphic persuasion.
Our Jane just went out for a mop,
But she got a romantic liaison.

And insect creations
Made their murmurations,
It wor t' first time o t' year to cast clout.
And ramblers wor rambling

And spring lambs wor gambolling
On t' day our Jane came out.

We wor all tucking into us teas,
When our Jane said, 'I've summat to say.'
As our kid trained his side eyes on me,
Jane stood up and told us, 'I'm gay.'

There wor birds celebrating
It wor their time for mating
And woodpeckers hammered it out.
And swallows wor soaring
And rivers stopped roaring
On t' day our Jane came out.

Mum went round to Gran's to explain.
She could see her mind having to grapple.
She said, 'A Wesleyan … our Jane?
But it's years since she's been to t' chapel!'

But she'd thrown off her stealth,
She wor being herself
As she walked into t' woods without doubt.
But near top o t' hill,
She froze … statue still …
On t' day our Jane came out.

She thought tarmac wor creeping up t' road,
She couldn't take in t' situation:
That hundreds of nut-brown toads
Wor making their annual migration.

But with nature in harmony,
She didn't harm any,
She didn't go hopping about!
As she carefully stepped,
Each small creature crept,
On t' day our Jane came out.

A Wolf wor down at t' stepping stones,
Mr B. B. Wolf to state fully.
He wor making low lascivious groans,
He wor t' mill owner's son an' a bully.

He said, 'What a nice meeting is this …
Why, it's t' fustian cutter's Daughter!
Give your Dad's old employer a kiss …
That's my price for you crossing this water.'

Jane said, 'I don't fancy your kiss, now you ask.
And I don't like your tone when you woo.
My lover is holding an axe,
And what's more, Mr Wolf … SHE'S BEHIND YOU!'

But that lass she met shoppin',
Whose job wor Woodchopping,
She didn't use her weapon or owt.
I hope you'll forgive her,
She pushed Wolf in t' river,
On t' day our Jane came out!

They walked back down t' Old Mill Road,
To t' Wishing Well, in t' Bluebell Copse,

When up hopped a frog …
An' up hopped a toad …
It wor' Wishing Well equal opps.

They said, 'cos none o t' toads had got squished,
Jane wor granted three wishes she wished!

She said, 'A sweetheart to marry me.'
(Though she thought that that could never be).
'And Hebden … t' Best Small Market Town …
Let's be …
An' t' Capital o t' North!'

Ms Toad asked Mr Frog, to read it all back from his Log.
He said, 'A sweetheart will marry thee … Rivet!
And Hebden: t' Best Small Market Town shall be … Rivet!
And t' Lesbian Capital o t' North. Knee deep!'

Though that third wish worn't as she'd intended,
Happen she wor glad it worn't amended …

'Cos, that's how it's all come about …
Since t' day our Jane came out!
Rivet!

Author's note: fairytales need a magical element and for me this
was provided by a walk in local woodlands when I encountered the
annual migration of tiny, nut brown toads (not the usual big mottled
ones we rescue in buckets from the path of local traffic). These
miniatures stopped their march when I stopped and started again
as I trod gingerly forward.

Mr E!

Said our Tourism Chief of renown,
When visitor numbers wor down,
Albert Einstein once stayed in this town.
He didn't!
He did.
He didn't!
He did. He wor at T' Grand View B&B.
He worn't!
He wor.
He worn't!
He wor. And t' locals called him Mr E.

But mainly he used his vacation
To work on his Special Equation.

What else did he do in these parts?
He wor a bit of a dab hand at darts.
He worn't!
He wor.
He worn't!
He wor. He scored a nine dart finish from t' ochie.
He didn't!
He did.
He didn't!
He did. For t' Railway against Horse and Jockey.
But mainly he used his vacation
To work on his Special Equation.

Mind – I only wish I'd had a ticket,
To watch Mr E playing cricket.
He didn't!
He did.
He didn't!
He did. He wor a spin bowling sensation.
He worn't!
He wor.
He worn't!
He wor …
Bamboozled batsmen wi' his oscillations.

And he went on long peregrinations,
To off beaten track destinations,
To work on his Special Equation.

Mind, he took in a Music Hall Show,
Emceed by a comedy duo.
And t' Straight Man – being more sage –
Got Mr E up on t' stage.

He admitted on sporting occasions
He made use of simple equations.
But all this wor just a rehearsal
For stating a Law Universal!

T' Comic MC said, 'By, he's clever!
He's got twice our brains put together!'
'BUT THAT'S IT!' Mr E declared …
And he points to himself …
Then he points to MC an' says …

He didn't!
He did.
He didn't!
He did.
He said, 'E EQUALS MC SQUARED!'

Author's note: 1905 was Einstein's 'miracle year' when he overturned existing notions of time and space and also took up darts.

Part Four: Cautionary Tales for Adolescents

Joan, who only had eyes for her phone and wor eaten …

Her Parents wor quite fond of Joan
And they bought her a Mobile Phone,
So she could do her Homework speedier,
Copying chunks from Wikipedia.
But Smartphones have magnetic powers,
Joan fiddled on her Phone for hours.
Until one day she wor offended,
On Facebook she had been Unfriended!
She screamed and shouted, 'It's not fair,
I wor just about to Unfriend her!'
Her Father pondered, 'What's to do?'
Till Mother said, 'Let's go to t' Zoo.'
And Father said, 'To enjoy us stay,
Put that blessed Phone away!'

For Joan had once loved Animals,
But sometimes childhood passion dulls.
She trudged through all t' best parts o t' Zoo,
Past Tiger, Lion, Kangaroo,
Whose glories wor all lost on Joan:
Who could not use her Mobile Phone!
But got revenge upon her Kin,
By looking miserable as sin.
Until, in t' Giant Reptile House –
Her Parents chatting Spouse to Spouse –
Through Jungle Ferns all dank with heat,
Joan sneaked off to send a tweet.

Extremely bored and overheated –
'I want my parents dead!' she tweeted –
With both eyes on her Phone she wandered,
On through steaming Jungle blundered.
Past DANGER! signs she did not see,
Alone at last and feeling free,
Till, by deep Pools – that smelt unhealthy –
She paused, to send her Friends a selfie.
When a hungry Crocodile – or perhaps it was an Alligator –
PHOTO BOMBED … then promptly ate Her!

Alerted by a noisy crunch
(A Reptile having Joan for Lunch)
The Zoo Keeper – a plucky feller –
Sacrificed his best Umbrella.
And propping open t' Creature's Jaws,
He dived Inside – to great applause!
For Joan's Father, a Cautious Chap,
Had bought a Phone Location App.
And t' Reptile's dark insides wor braved …
And t' Smartphone, though not Joan, wor saved!

So think on: put down that Phone –
Or else you might end up like Joan!

Author's note: these tales are inspired by Hilaire Belloc's
Cautionary Tales for posh Edwardian children and his parodies
of Victorian morality tales – including the mock archaic over
employment of Capital Letters!
Michael, who always made a mess, but now his family are one
less

Michael, like some other Boys,
Never tidied up his Toys!
And Outside, when eating Sweets,
Threw his Wrappers down in t' Streets!

And he became an Uncouth Youth,
His Sweetheart Vickie wor far more Couth,
But country walking, her pet Lulu
Made a Pile of Doggy Do Do!

With Special Glove on, swift and deft,
She scooped it up till none wor left.
But in a test of Michael's love,
She handed him that special Glove!

Now some way off there wor a Bin,
For putting Doggy Do Do in,
But Michael hoped for a canoodle,
Not Doggy Do Do from a Poodle!

So he reached up and brazenly,
Hung that Do Do from a Tree!
This act wor seen by Farmer Kath,
Who muttered, 'That Michael's having a laugh!'

Now on patrol it wor Kath's habit,
To take a Gun to shoot at Rabbits.
She didn't want young Michael dead –
But FIRED A SHOT above his head!

Then, back down t' Hill ran Little Lulu –
And Vickie raced to catch her Poodle –
But Michael ran and jumped in t' Bin,
Where folks put Doggy Do Do in!

When by a Great Coincidence,
(T' odds on which wor quite Immense),
Bin Men drove up! Young and Strong,
And didn't hang about for long.

For they'd been parked up, reading T' Sun,
And thought Kath fired at them wit' Gun!
They hoisted t' Bin up Double-Smart,
And tipped its contents in their Cart.

Then they drove off, past Dog and Vickie,
Who shouted, 'Stop! You're taking Micky!'
In t' back o t' Dust Cart, Michael stirred
And shouted t' English word for Merde!

But in that Dust Cart, high spec kit
Chewed up Michael, BIT by BIT!
And at a Land-fill, where they Recycle,
Dumped three parts Do Do to two parts Michael.

His Parents said, 'Well, we're one Lad fewer …
But at least he'll make a good Manure!'

Damien, who cheeked his elders, but … Damien ended up in t' Cut!

Damien had one Great Defect,
He Showed his Elders No Respect.
At Secondary School, it's sad to mention,
How often Damien wor on Detention.
He tried to get more Friends, alas,
By being t' Biggest Clown in t' Class …
That Whoopee Cushion on a Chair,
On Speech Day: Damien put it there.
And Damien proved himself a chump
By causing t' Lady Mayor to trump!

But imagine a POET, most August,
(Take a moment, if you must),
Strolling along, taking his time …
Antennae tuned into t' sublime …
Sucking upon a Haliborange,
Whilst trying to find a rhyme for orange …
Enjoying that scene he loved so well,
T' towpath on t' Rochdale Canal,
When out of Nowhere – You Know Who –
Damien leapt out, shouting, 'WHOOOH!'

He hoped he'd make his Friends all laugh –
Poppy, Gaz and Gorgeous Kath –
For Damien thought this frightful Din
Would make our Bard jump out o t' Skin!
Only to find, to his distress,
Our Poet wor once in t' S.A.S!

And Damien's plight wor quite precarious,
That Poet wor tuned like a Stradivarius!
He'd been a Soldier and then a Spy,
And that is the reason why –
Although he wor four decades older –
He THREW young Damien over t' shoulder!

And, Somersaulting through t' air, he Fell
Wit' giant SPLASSSHHH! into t' Canal.
And, after a few moments pause,
Our Poet's ears filled with Applause!
For Damien's Mates, as youngsters can,
Felt Great Respect for that Old Man,
Who Smiled at them and blew a Kiss,
Then wondered off, in t' State of Bliss.
Could this be True? Who wor this Fella?
Friends! It wor ME, your Storyteller!

So Remember Damien, (I think you'd better),
A little Wiser, but so much Wetter!

Author's note: inspired by a real encounter on a towpath – the rest
of the tale is also true.

Songs

Introduction: Our Percy

(spoken introduction)

Eee … I'm worried about our Percy,
I'm reet worried about our Perce.
Since joining that storytelling club
He's been under some sort of curse.
First off he wor telling monologues
And allus talking in verse.
But now he's bought a weskit
And he's taken a turn for t' worst.
He's started singing folksongs!
Oh, where did we go wrong?
He stands there with his hand to his ear,
And wants us to sing along!
We allus did us best by t' lad,
Since he took his first breath.
We played him tunes by t' Sex Pistols
And such as Megadeath.
But just to put a cap on things,
He's bought a ukulele!
It must have cost him twenty pounds,
And he's plucking on it daily!
Father says, 'Don't worry Mother.
I'm sure he'll soon get bored.
He's been plucking it for a fortnight now,
And he's not mastered plucking t' first chord!'

Fancy Man Stan

I'll tell thee a tale of a singular man –
Stan, Stan, Fancy Man Stan.
For wooing of widows wor his secret plan –
Stan, Stan, Fancy Man Stan.
His voice like molasses
And golden his tan,
He didn't chase lasses …
He went after grans!
And soon a rich widow wor his biggest fan –
Stan, Stan, Fancy Man Stan.

She gave him employment as her handyman –
Stan, Stan, Fancy Man Stan.
And hands on enjoyment wor part of her plan –
For Stan, Stan, Fancy Man Stan.
An' when that Old Dame
Shuffled off t' mortal coil,
He'd ten grand to his name
When he laid her in t' soil!
And that's how t' pursuit of rich widows began
By Stan, Stan, Fancy Man Stan.

To prove that first conquest worn't just flash in t' pan –
For Stan, Stan, Fancy Man Stan,
Next widow he courted wor Dowager Anne!
Stan, Stan, Fancy Man Stan.
At t' art of love making
He wor a magician –
For he got parts working

Long out of commission!
And she changed her will
And got reading o t' banns –
For Stan, Stan, Fancy Man Stan.

But soon after her church weddin' began,
To Stan, Stan, Fancy Man Stan.
A furious woman across that church ran –
At Stan, Stan, Fancy Man Stan.
And her voice rang out hard …
In its echoing strife –
'Stop this charade –
For I'm your true wife!'
And all stood like statues – except for one man –
Stan, Stan, Fancy Man Stan!

So off into legend that bad rascal ran –
Stan, Stan, Fancy Man Stan.
For wooing of widows wor his secret plan –
Stan, Stan Fancy Man Stan.
For he had a scheme,
When digging for gold,
To help women dream
They'd never grow old!
An' that's how he made them change their pension plans!
Stan, Stan, Fancy Man Stan!

It's Grim Down South

(To the tune of My Bonnie Lies Over the Ocean)

A dusting of snow lies on Surrey,
With drifts almost half an inch deep.
And London has had a light flurry –
Now rush hour's been slowed to a creep.
Up north our bad weather's more chronic,
But we never get reet down in t' mouth
(Down in t' mouth)
If we utter these words as a tonic:
Eee but it's grim down south!

(Chorus)
Eee but …
Eee but …
Eee but it's grim down south, down south!
Eee but …
Eee but …
Eee but it's grim down south!
An' we dance t' hootchy cooch,
North of Ashby de la Zouch,
Singin' Eee but it's grim down south!

And when Pennine snow's piled up to t' windows,
But TV News don't want to know,
'Cos backroom Nigels an' Belindas
Say ours isn't 'The right type of snow.'
We summon our humour sardonic,
From Merseyside up to Tynemouth

(To Tynemouth)
Though our heating bill's grown astronomic,
We say, 'Eee but it's grim down south!'

(Chorus)

Winter's long, but we'll get through it,
If we think on t' Inuit,
An' sing 'Eee but it's grim down south!'

I wor tawkin' 'bout fundin' of London
An' all t' capital t' capital takes,
When a mate who's a London offcumden,
Said, 'They've not got your hills and lakes.'
And I dreamt 'bout this new high speed rail,
And all t' passengers sang with one mouth
(With one mouth)
As their train left King's Cross they all wail:
'Eee but it's grim down south!'

(Chorus)

And as they ride forth to t' glories up north,
They sing, Eee but it's grim down south!

Home for Christmas

Oh they told me, 'Home for Christmas'
When they took my name from me.
When I told them I'm an orphan,
Said, 'We're your family.
But if there's a miss you'll miss,
Better leave her name.
Tell her, you'll be home for Christmas,'
And I thought of you, Elaine.

[Slow repeated drum phrase]

And I thought I saw you running,
As we marched towards the train.
And the drums were slowly drumming
To the patter of the rain,
And you raised your lips to kiss,
'Fore we moved away.
And you told me, 'Home for Christmas!'
As I waved to you, Elaine.

[Drumming]

And the ship's engines were churning
To the beat of that refrain,
And I thought of all the sailors
Lying deep beneath the main.
And their voices whispered
Like a chorus of the slain,
Telling me, 'Be home for Christmas,'
Like a mantra for the slain.

[Drumming: rising in volume to final emphatic beat]

And the bullet was a greeting
Sent by a stranger's hand.
And again I am an orphan,
Lying here in no-man's-land.
And my last wish is to kiss you again,
But the drums are slowly fading
As I think of you, Elaine.

[Drumming: quieter and fractured as it fades out]

Author's note: inspired by a 1914 photograph of soldiers starting
the march from Stubbing Wharf in Hebden Bridge to Todmorden
Railway Station for the journey to France. I realised I had never read
a story of orphan soldiers.

Marjory Dexter, School's Inspector

(OFSTED, the schools inspectorate, have dropped the grade of 'Satisfactory' and replaced it with 'Must Improve'. I wonder how this would work in other areas of life …)

[To the tune of the Pizzicati from the ballet Sylvia by Delibes]

Richard Perkins, most parts working,
Looking for late romance joined a dating agency.
Met Marjory Dexter, Schools Inspector,
She gave ratings after datings in five categories …

[Female part]
Your manners and opinions I endorse: Grade 4s!
Your country house and cars deserve applause: more 4s!
But sex was only Satisfactory: Grade 3!
So really, Richard, don't start boasting,
Friends agree that you've been coasting,
On this website I am hosting!

If we should date again by any chance, Dickie!
You really ought to think of ambience, Dickie!
So stir my fires down below,
You'll never make my embers glow,
By playing tracks by Barry Manilow, Dickie!

[Male part]
Marjory Dexter, Schools Inspector,
Thank you for your ratings in all five categories.
You say our mating was deflating,
Satisfaction calls for action, but you're hard to please.

Although your charms I find hard to resist, Marjory!
Every move I made you ticked a list, Marjory!
And then you put on t' Ride o t' Valkyries, Marjory!
And it did not increase my pleasure,
Contemplating parts I treasure,
When you took out your Tape Measure!
Your website says that you admire restraint, Marjory!
But when I saw your whips I felt quite faint, Marjory!
At bravery I'm not a champ,
I draw the line at Nipple Clamps,
In fact, I'm Satisfied I scored Grade 3, Marjory!

21st Century Man

I'll tell a tale that starts with ale,
One night I came in from the pub
And found a note that said, 'Dear John,
You've joined the Singles Club!
I'm sorry John, I've left you.
I've found my Special One.
And everyone, except you,
Has known that I've been "Carrying On"
With Tony, don't phone me,
We're touring in a Campervan.
And as we watch the seasons go,
He'll help my memories to Grow,
'Cause he's a late-blooming, Baby Booming,
21st Century Man!

(Chorus)
Hold hands, last stand,
Living till we drop.
Lad, lass, Bus Pass,
Till the bell rings: Your Stop!

My Wife had left, and so bereft,
I quit the telly and the pub.
A hand above gave me a shove
To the 3rd Age Social Club.
My favourite night was Tuesday,
When we did Free Form Dance.
And in "Ladies' Excuse Me,"
I often thought I'd have a chance,

With Maureen, Doreen,
Susie, Cynthia or Jan.
And as we watched the seasons go,
They'd help my memories to grow.
I'd be a late blooming, Baby Booming,
21st Century Man!

(Chorus)
Hold hands, last stand,
Living till we drop
Lad, lass, Bus Pass,
Till the bell rings: Your Stop!

Don't try to ring me, Maria.
You chose your Mother to see.
Since then you've hardly been near:
You'll not get a penny from me!

Now my best bet, wor t' internet,
I set myself up with a hub,
And using Skype, found just my type,
At the World-Wide Dating Club.
And now she's my fiancé,
Although she's half my age.
She looks just like Beyoncé.
I help to supplement her wage.
Niagara, Viagra, a honeymoon is in the plan.
And as we watch the seasons go,
She'll help my memories to grow.
I'll be a late blooming, Baby Booming,
21st Century Man!

(Chorus)
Hold hands, last stand,
Living till we drop.
Lad, lass, Bus Pass
Till the bell rings: Your Stop!

Author's note: a widower I know was told by his son that he would never speak to him again if he married his new Thai partner because this meant he would lose his inheritance.

Le Grand Depart (or, Mrs Pomfret's Pomme Frites)

(Sung words shown in italics)

T' officials at Tour de France bike race,
Said they'd run out of roads around France.
So our tourism chap, with a straight face,
Said, 'Why not give Yorkshire a chance!'

(Chorus)
Oh, when we had our Grand Depart –
On your bikes, au revoir, big tara –
Le peloton went past in a glance,
Some folks took t' chance
For a weekend romance,
But we all said that Yorkshire wor t' star,
When we had our Grand Depart.

All t' lamp posts wor bendin' wi' bunting
And skies wor all cloudless and blue.
And yellow bikes hung from t' shops frontin'
On t' streets where t' big bike race wor due.
And Mrs Veronica Pomfret – casting off her widow's kit –
Frenchified her pub menu
For passin' French men who
Might fancy their Cod Piece on a bed of Pomme Frites!

(Chorus)

Well, he stood out in t' crowd, bronzed and healthy,
Till someone said, 'Here's t' peloton!'

Then Bernard, turned round for a selfie,
But when he turned back t' bikes had gone!
So he walked on to t' pub in his beret,
With his hooped shirt an' handlebar 'tache.
Though he looked like a cliché, from t' Champs Elysee,
Mrs Pomfret admired his Gallic panache!

(Chorus)

That night wor our Anglo – French Ball,
An' we all wore celebrity masks.
T' French DJ wor General De Gaulle,
Alan Bennett played all t' English tracks.
An' we danced to La vie en Rosie
An' boogied to Bat out of Hell,
No one noticed our pair,
As they slipped upstairs:
Nora Batty with Sacha Distel!

(Chorus)

Oh my Veronique, Yorkshire's magnifique,
Across those contours I would be a wanderer.
I would spend an hour at your Lady Bower,
Your hills and dales double entendre!

Then he drove her to un, deux, trois peaks …!
Smoked an E cigarette an' then
She lay in his arms, cheek to chic,
Sayin' 'Je ne regrette rien!'
But after t' Depart, he sent a post card

An' she wor surprised what he put:
He said, 'I'm not Bernard
From south of Dinard …
I'm Bernard from Luddenden Foot!'

(Chorus)

Author's note: I spotted Bernard in the crowd during day two of the 2014 Tour de France when it passed by our house.

End Piece: The Near Future

Android Hospital

Some o t' lads went to t' Android Hospital,
It wor set in t' near future, not far.
There wor Maurice, our John, and young Jamie,
And they went in a driverless car.

Now Maurice had an ingrowing toenail
And young Jamie had signed up for t' snip,
And our John, he wor after a bionic foot,
To go wi' his bionic hip.

These treatments wor proper expensive,
But they've managed to claim t' money back,
Cos' that night they went down to t' theatres
Wor t' night o t' cyber attack!

When Maurice came out of sedation,
His foot wor quite pain free; although,
When he took his surgical sock off
He found he wor minus one toe …

And our John, who wor one for his dancing,
A dapper old gent, quite sweet.
Has had to give up on his hobby,
Now he's literally got two left feet …

But I won't hear a word against androids,
It's humans as wants to attack us –
An' t' surgeons at t' Android Hospital
Had their programs hacked into by hackers!

But spare a thought for young Jamie,
His treatment's quite scrambled his head.
He went in for a vasectomy,
But he got a vagina instead!

Author's note: I was writing this tale when the news overtook me, in the form of a cyber attack on targets around the globe, including hospital computers in the UK.

About the Author

George Murphy is a performance storyteller with a rich and varied body of published works to his name. As this book was in production, his folktales for African schoolchildren (in the Macmillan Reading World series) had sold over 130,000 copies.

He first became interested in performance storytelling when he attended a workshop in Halifax in 1989. The tales he told and wrote appeared in Betty Rosen's Shapers and Polishers (Mary Glasgow Publications).

After 20 years teacher training he co-edited, with his colleague Maggie Power, A Tale to Tell (Trentham) about storytelling in primary schools. Since retirement, George has been writing and performing comic monologues and songs for adult audiences, sometimes alongside Rod Dimbleby in The Rod and George Show. People have paid to laugh at him all over the North – and even as far south as Nottingham!

He has also served time in an 'Education Think Tank', done research for BBC Scotland, been lead singer in a rock band, a chorister in G&S productions and – in his far off youth – represented Cheshire Schools, Yorkshire and The North of England at middle and long distances.

George has been a committee member of Shaggy Dog Storytellers for many years. He has recently joined Hebden Bridge Ukulele Jam, and practices diligently – well out of ear shot of his wife!

He maintains a website at irregular intervals: Murphy's Monologues on georgemurphysite.wordpress.com

Many of these tales have appeared in an ebook version in association with HebWeb and Pennine publications.

For bookings and other matters contact George via georgestories@icloud.com

If you have enjoyed this book, please consider leaving a review for George on Amazon and Goodreads to let him know what you thought of his work.

You can find out more about George on his author page on the Fantastic Books Store. While you're there, why not browse our other delightful tales and wonderfully woven prose?

www.fantasticbooksstore.com

47210294R00059

Printed in Poland
by Amazon Fulfillment
Poland Sp. z o.o., Wrocław